Barbro Lindgren

THE STORY OF THE LITTLE OLD MAN

ILLUSTRATIONS BY
Eva Eriksson

Translated by
Steven T. Murray

R&S
BOOKS

Stockholm New York London Adelaide Toronto

Rabén & Sjögren   Stockholm

Translation copyright © 1991 by Rabén & Sjögren
All rights reserved
Illustrations copyright © 1979 by Eva Eriksson
Originally published in Sweden under the title
Sagan om den lilla farbrorn,
text copyright © 1979 by Barbro Lindgren
Library of Congress catalog card number: 91-60101
Printed in Sweden
First edition, 1992

ISBN 91-29-59942-3

R & S Books are distributed in the United States of America
by Farrar, Straus and Giroux, New York;
in the United Kingdom by Ragged Bears, Andover;
in Canada by Vanwell Publishing, St. Catharines;
and in Australia by ERA Publications, Adelaide

Once upon a time, there was a little old man. He was a very lonely little old man. Nobody liked him, even though he was very nice. They thought he was too little. And they thought he looked much too silly.

And they thought his hat was
ugly, too.

That's why everybody was mean
to the little old man.

It did no good for him to keep
tipping his hat to say hello. Nobody
liked him anyway.

The dogs would growl at him, and
the old men would trip him when he
went out for his morning stroll.

At night, the little old man would lie in bed crying because he was so lonely.

Why doesn't anyone like me? I'm so nice, he thought.

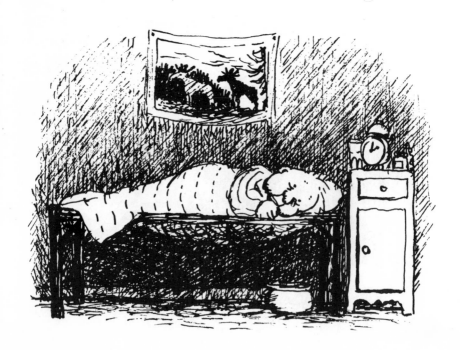

One day, just as spring arrived, he
went outside and put up signs on the
trees. On the signs he wrote:

LONELY LITTLE OLD MAN IS LOOKING
FOR A FRIEND

And then he wrote his name and
his address.

He sat down on his steps and
waited. He waited and waited. For
ten days and ten nights, he waited.
In the daytime the sun was shining,
and the first snowdrops pushed their
way up out of the ground.

At night, the blackbirds would sing so beautifully that it made him cry.

But nobody wanted to be his friend. They all pretended not to see the little old man on the steps.

On the tenth night, the little old man got tired and dozed off for a while. And suddenly ...

a cold nose in his hand woke him
up. Beside him sat a big dog with his
tail in an elegant curl.

The big dog gave him such a nice look and laid his heavy head on the little old man's shoulder.

The little old man was so happy that he fell over backwards.

The dog thought that was funny.

As soon as the little old man sat down on the steps again, the dog laid his head on the little old man's shoulder – and *ka-chong*! he fell over backwards again.

The little old man thought it was fun to fall over. He hadn't fallen over in forty years! (At least, not backwards.)

It was still night outside.

The blackbirds were singing their hearts out, and three stars were blinking in the sky.

The little old man went into the kitchen and got four cookies.

The dog ate them up in five
seconds.

He licked the little old man from
his shoes all the way up to his hat.

Then he wagged his tail and
walked away.
"Come back tomorrow," said the
little old man.

The next day, the little old man
was sitting on the steps with eight
cookies in his pocket. The sun was
shining that day, too, and the
blackbirds were pulling worms out
of the ground.

All of a sudden, the old man felt a cold nose in his hand. The dog had come back!

The old man took the cookies out of his pocket, and the dog almost fainted from happiness.

They sat on the steps for the rest of the day. The dog kept his nose in the little old man's hand. And the little old man sat as quiet as a mouse, so the nose would stay there.

When evening came, the dog got up and walked away.

"Come back tomorrow," said the little old man.

The next morning, he was sitting
on his steps with twelve cookies in
his pocket.

Now all the tulips had opened up,
and the blackbirds were flying
around with twigs in their mouths.

At ten o'clock, the dog showed up.
In eleven seconds he ate up the
twelve cookies. Then he was so full
that he fell asleep.

When night came, he woke up and walked away.

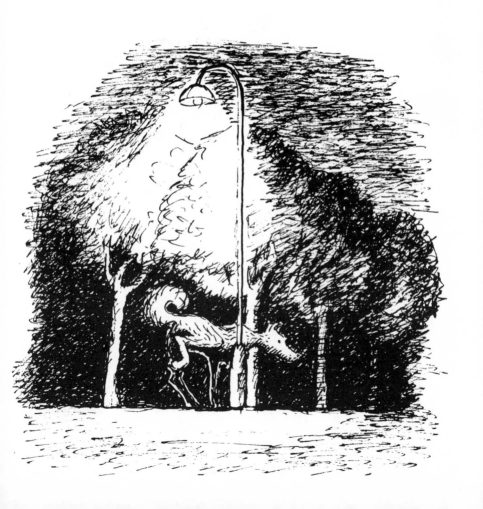

But the next morning, when the little old man opened his door, the dog was already standing there. His mouth was full of old bones and sticks.

The little old man was filled with joy.

"Come in," he said, opening the door.

First the dog came into the kitchen. There he put his bones and sticks under the table.

Then he ate up the little old man's food. The little old man was *so* glad that the dog wanted to eat his food.

In the evening, the dog went into the bedroom. He lay down right away in the little old man's bed. The little old man was *so* glad that the dog wanted to sleep in his bed. The little old man slept on the floor in a box.

The next morning, the cowslips had bloomed, too, and the blackbirds were laying eggs in their nests.

The dog and the little old man woke up at the same instant. They sat up and looked at each other in surprise.

Of course! I've got a friend now, thought the little old man.

Of course! I've got a little old man now, thought the dog.

Later they went out for a walk in the sunshine. The dog sniffed at trees and the little old man sniffed at flowers.

All of a sudden, a mean old man came and tripped the little old man.

He didn't know that the dog and the little old man were friends. Just as the little old man fell to the ground, the dog came racing up.

Oh, how scared the mean old man was!

He ran for his life. The dog and the little old man had to sit down on the grass and laugh.

When they were finished laughing,
a mean dog came out of the bushes
and growled at the little old man. He
didn't know either that the little old
man and the big dog were friends.

When the big dog came rushing at
him, the mean dog got terribly
scared. He rolled over on his back
and howled like a cat.

Oh, how the little old man and the
big dog laughed!

That's how the days passed. The trees got greener and greener. The little old man and the dog got happier and happier. It turned into summer.

In the evenings, they would sit on the steps and think. The little old man thought about life and about how much fun it is to have a friend.

The big dog thought about holes and about how good bones are.

On Sundays, the little old man brought a box home from the bakery. On Thursdays, they ate pea soup with ham.

Autumn came. The leaves fell from the trees, and the blackbirds flew south.

But the old man and the dog took out a blanket and kept sitting on the steps, thinking about life and watching everyone who passed by.

Winter came. So they went inside, because it was too cold on their behinds.

But when spring came again, they
went back outside.

3

One day, a little girl came hopping
through the puddles. She was a
sweet little girl, with a polka-dot
dress, and a bow in her hair.

The girl sat down on the steps and leaned against the dog. The dog shivered with happiness and moved his nose to the girl's hand instead of the little old man's.

The little old man got a twinge in his chest and the world turned blurry around him. He sat at the far edge of the steps and looked away.

4

The next day, the girl came back
and sat down close to the dog. Then
the little old man went away and
cried. His tears dropped like pearls
onto the moss. And he thought about
the steps and the dog and about the
nose that used to rest in his hand.

But when he thought about the
other little hand, he was filled with
sorrow and sadness.

The dog doesn't like me anymore,
he thought. He likes the little girl
better. Because she is little and
sweet and I'm little and ugly!

For seven days, the dog and the girl sat on the steps and wondered where the little old man had gone.

And for seven days, the little old
man walked in the woods and cried.
But on the eighth day, he came back
to see whether the dog and the girl
were still sitting there.

Yes, the dog was sitting there, and
the girl was sitting there, too. And
the dog's head was drooping like a
withered tulip.

But when he saw the little old
man, he became wild with joy and
came rushing toward him.

The little old man and the dog fell into each other's arms. And the girl danced and clapped her hands. At the same instant, the snowdrops burst open and the blackbirds came flying down and started pulling worms out of the ground.

The little old man felt warm with happiness.

Then they sat down on the steps, just as before. The dog put his nose in the little old man's hand. And the girl put her hand in his other one.

And the little old man never had to feel lonely again.

DATE		

BAKER & TAYLOR BOOKS